For Penny
DM

To all those who keep my heart dancing.
Life is so much better because of you!
RF

And for all children everywhere
DM and RF

Text copyright © 2021 by David Martin
Illustrations copyright © 2021 by Raissa Figueroa

First edition 2021

Library of Congress Catalog Card Number pending
ISBN 978-1-5362-0918-1

21 22 23 24 25 26 TLF 10 9 8 7 6 5 4 3 2 1

Printed in Dongguan, Guangdong, China

This book was typeset in Billy.
The illustrations were created digitally.

Candlewick Press
99 Dover Street
Somerville, Massachusetts 02144

www.candlewick.com

The More the Merrier

David Martin

illustrated by Raissa Figueroa

CANDLEWICK PRESS

HEY, HEY, here comes Bear—

Over rocks, under trees,
Kicking feet, bending knees,

stepping high, stepping low,

stepping fast, stepping slow.

And he's not alone, or not for long.
Loose as a goose . . .

It's Moose!

"I like your moves. But I'm not like you.
So I'll just do what I can do."

Galumphing high, galumphing low,

Galumphing fast, galumphing slow.

Next, out of hiding,
Slipping and sliding . . .

It's Snake!

"I like your steps. But I'm not like you.
So I'll just do what I can do."

Wiggling high, wiggling low,

Wiggling fast, wiggling slow.

But we're not done.
Jumping in, just for fun . . .

It's Deer!

"I like your beat. But I'm not like you.
So I'll just do what I can do."

Leaping high, leaping low,

Leaping fast, leaping slow.

Then, seeing all with big, round eyes,
Swooping down—a silent surprise . . .

It's Owl!

"Hey, your be-bop swings. But I'm not like you.
So I'll just do what I can do."

Flying high, flying low,

Flying fast, flying slow.

And guess who's next . . .

It's Baby Mouse!

"Me too! Me too!
Watch me do what I can do."

Skipping high, skipping low,

Skipping fast, skipping slow.

Then Mouse's friends come
On the run,
Singing, "Hey diddle, diddle,
That looks like fun."

Chirping, cheeping,
Barking, peeping—
The more the merrier.

Then all in a circle, around they go: stepping high, galumphing low,

leaping fast, wiggling slow, skippity-skipping, flappity-flipping . . .

Every voice,
Low to high,
Singing to trees,
Singing to sky,
Until they collapse
In a heap,
Laughing and laughing . . .

Until they're asleep

Together.